BIGMAMA

Harbor
Donald Crews

Greenwillow Books, New York

BIGMAMA

CEMENT CEMENT

electronic or
mechanical, including
photocopying,
recording or by any
information storage
and retrieval system,
without permission
in writing from the
Publisher,
Greenwillow Books,
a division of William
Morrow & Company,
Inc., 105 Madison Ave.,
New York, N.Y. 10016.

Printed in the United
States of America
First Edition
10 9 8 7 6 5 4 3

Library of Congress
Cataloging in
Publication Data

Crews, Donald. Harbor.
Summary: Presents
various kinds of
boats which come and
go in a busy harbor.
1. Ships—Pictorial
works—Juvenile
literature.
[1. Harbors. 2. Boats] I. Title.
VM307.C8   623.8'2'00222   81-6607
ISBN 0-688-00861-5   AACR2
ISBN 0-688-00862-3 (lib. bdg.)

To the women in my life
& Malcolm

A harbor.

Wharves, docks, piers, and warehouses.

A port for ships,
boats, and cargo.

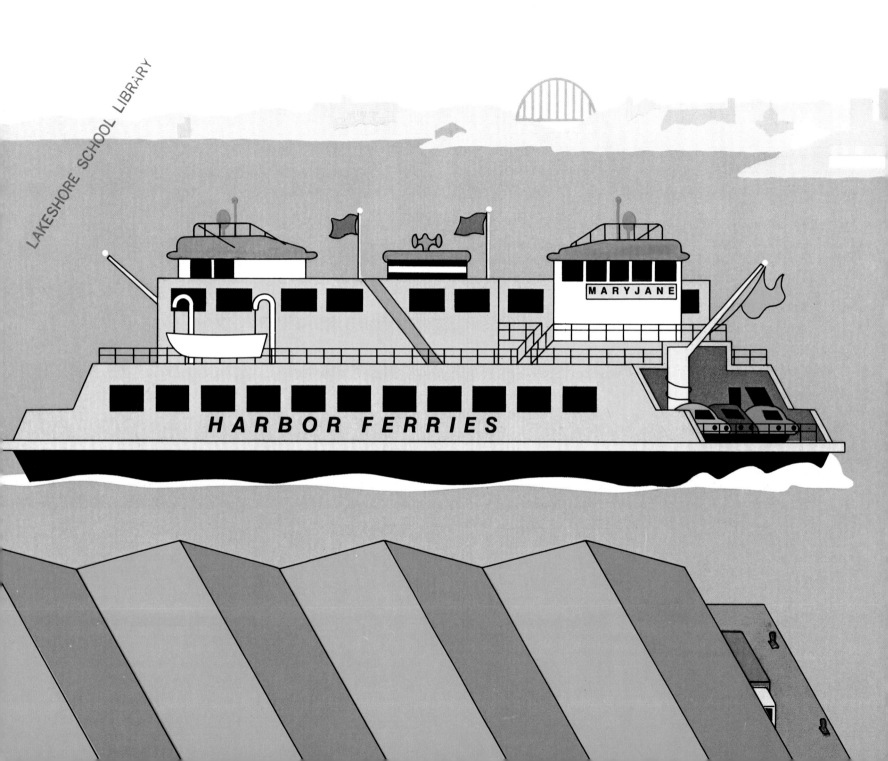

HARBOR FERRIES

MARYJANE

**Ferryboats shuttle back and forth
from shore to shore.
They do not need to turn around.
The back becomes the front.**

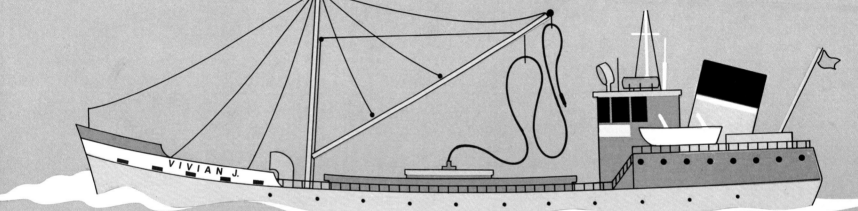

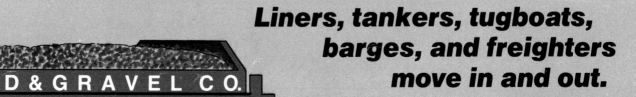

Liners, tankers, tugboats, barges, and freighters move in and out.

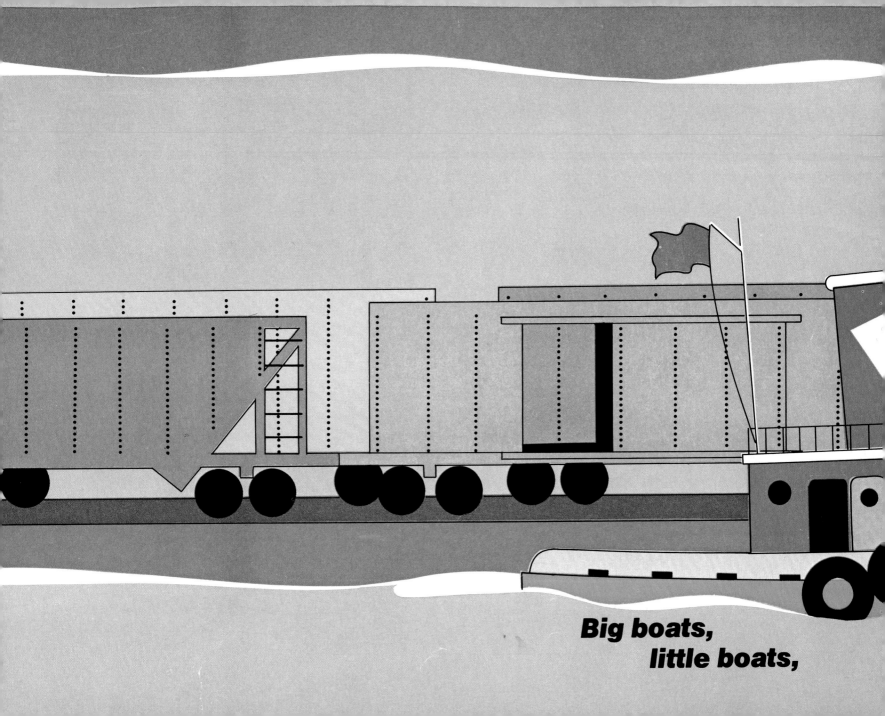

Big boats,
little boats,

long, low-lying barges,

fast police boats, and
slow-moving lighters
crowd the water.

The tugboat is the busiest boat in the harbor.

Tugs push.
Tugs tow.

*Tugs guide big boats
to their docks*

MALCOLM

AVA

and out again.

**In the harbor the fireboat
is ready for an emergency**

or a celebration.

Ship Shapes

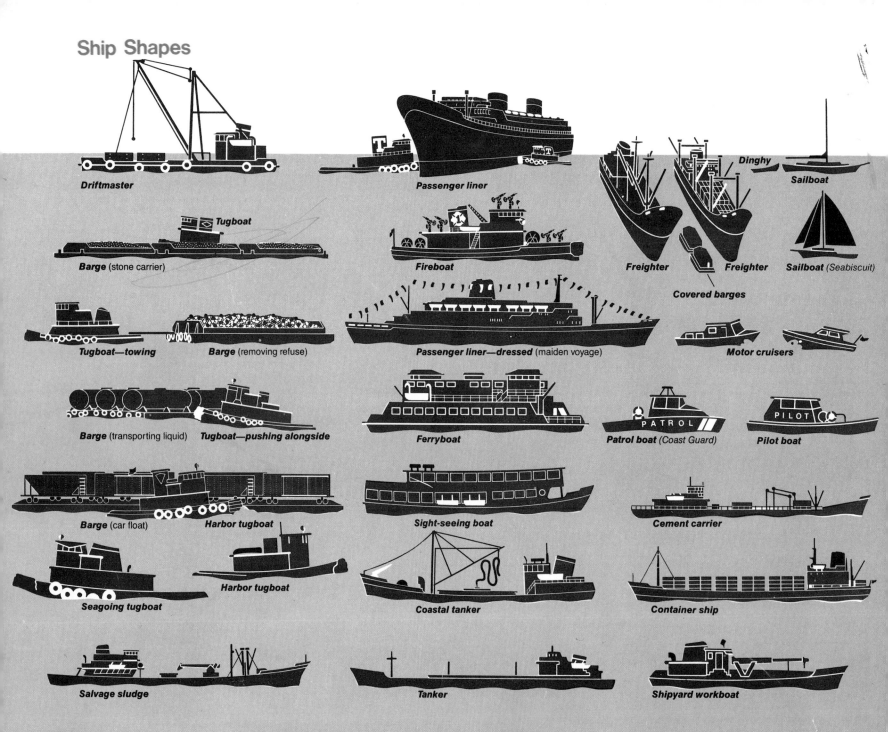

Driftmaster

Passenger liner

Dinghy

Sailboat

Tugboat

Barge (stone carrier)

Fireboat

Freighter **Freighter**

Sailboat (Seabiscuit)

Covered barges

Tugboat—towing **Barge** (removing refuse)

Passenger liner—dressed (maiden voyage)

Motor cruisers

Barge (transporting liquid) **Tugboat—pushing alongside**

Ferryboat

Patrol boat (Coast Guard)

PATROL

Pilot boat

PILOT

Barge (car float) **Harbor tugboat**

Sight-seeing boat

Cement carrier

Harbor tugboat

Seagoing tugboat

Coastal tanker

Container ship

Salvage sludge

Tanker

Shipyard workboat